# Other Children's Book Recommendation

Look inside ↓

Look inside ↓

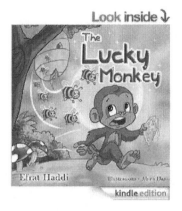

Look inside ↓

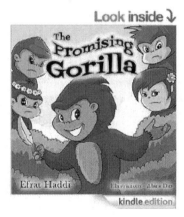

Look inside ↓

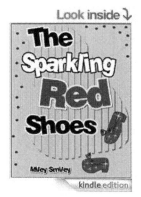

The Sparkling Red Shoes

Miley Smiley

kindle edition

Why do turtles have a Shell? NEW

By S. Adler

Illustrated by Abira Das

kindle edition

Unique in a Wonderful Way

WRITTEN BY KATE HART
ILLUSTRATED BY JASMINE MILLS

kindle edition

Abigail AND THE NORTH POLE ADVENTURE

Written by Tali Carmi

Illustrated by Neda Pschedarieva

kindle edition

# NEW RELEASE

# THE CLUEFINDERS CLUB STORY 1

## —THE CASE OF THE— VANISHING BULLY

HELP TRAIN YOUR CHILDREN'S IMAGINATION

Beatrix didn't like school. She was only twelve, just like all her friends, and she truly believed she'd never hated anything so much.

The reason she hated school was because she got bullied.

Her Mum told her that she should just ignore bullies at school, because usually they were scared and simple on the inside, even if they were big and tough on the outside. With a little compassion, they might learn to be nicer people. Her Dad told her to be strong and give as good as she got. "If one of those prissy prom queens gives you a hard time, just knock her on in the nose!"

Beatrix didn't think doing anything to anyone's nose would help the situation. Besides, she was smart enough to know that violence was rarely the answer. But her Mum's advice was hardly helpful either. What was she supposed to do?

The prime bully was called Tania. Tania was in the year above Beatrix, and two inches taller. She usually wore her hair in a pony tail, and had braces on her teeth that glinted evilly whenever she sneered, which was often. Tania was not very clever, and always did poorly in class. She had been known to throw her text book onto the floor whenever a question was too tough for her. Her pencil case would fly off the desk, scattering pens and pencils across the classroom.

The teachers were never very happy with Tania, or her two best friends, Jada and Juliet. The three of them were usually put in detention together to teach them a lesson, so to speak. But it never seemed to work: the very next lunchtime, they would be up to their usual tricks, terrorizing smaller children in the playground.

Beatrix considered herself a nicer child, and because she was nice, she had many friends. Her three best friends were Clara, Christopher and Benjamin – or Ben for short. The four of them had been good friends ever since the first day of school. Chris often said, "I bet we'll be friends forever – even when we're old and grey-haired!"

Beatrix hoped so. There weren't many things that made her so happy as spending time with her friends.

One day, at school, Tania the bully was being particularly mean. She, Jada and Juliet had cornered Beatrix in the yard.

"Give us your lunch money!" demanded Tania, holding out her hand. She always painted her fingernails in many different colours, which Beatrix thought was stupid.

"No!" said Beatrix. Why should she give away her lunch money and go hungry, just because Tania's mother always gave her a rubbish packed lunch to eat every day?

"If you don't," said Tania, "then I'm going to hurt you. Really bad. And then everyone will see you crying!"

Beatrix was afraid. And she was already close to crying. But she didn't want to give the bullies the satisfaction of seeing her that way, so she held back her tears and refused to part with her lunch money.

Just as Tania was about to get violent, Beatrix was saved! Ben, Chris and Clara came running over from the yard, where they had been playing. "Leave Beatrix alone!" shouted Clara.

It seemed that there was no choice but to fight.

Luckily, their teacher, Mister Faraday, had seen the trouble brewing through the classroom window, and now strode out like a giant to confront them.

"Miss Mackendale!" he said, which was Tania's surname. When he was angry, he always referred to the children by their surnames. "I heard everything you said. Go to the detention room – now!"

Tania complained, but it was no use. This time, they'd been caught!

"Are you okay?" Mister Faraday asked Beatrix. "Did they hurt you?"

"No, you were just in time. Thank you!"

The teacher wore glasses. He also had a big moustache on his top lip. He wiggled his moustache and pushed his glasses up his nose. "If you ever have trouble with another pupil, you just come to me, okay? It's a shame that the good ones have to suffer because of the bad ones, but sometimes this is how it is."

Tania was put into the detention room, which was a small classroom where a teacher watched over the naughty child until the end of lunchtime. Their punishment was that they couldn't play outside with their friends. Jada and Juliet talked their way out of it – they said that Tania *made* them be mean. Mister Faraday couldn't be sure that they weren't lying, so he let them go. But Tania had to stay in the detention room for the rest of lunchtime. Mister Faraday sat outside the room in a chair and read his book.

When the bell rang for the end of lunchtime, Beatrix, Ben, Clara and Chris stopped playing football together and went back inside to class. They walked right past the detention room, where Mister Faraday's nose was stuck in his book. He looked up, surprised.

"Oh, is it class time already? I'd better let Tania out. I hope she's learned her lesson about being unkind."

He opened the door – but the room was empty!

Tania had disappeared!

"What's going on here?" Mister Faraday cried.

They all went into the detention room. There was the empty teacher's desk, and four empty smaller desks for naughty students. Tania had been sitting in the first one, but she wasn't there now!

Mister Faraday checked the window, which was locked from the inside. He looked in the store cupboard, where the text books were kept, and it was empty. There seemed no explanation for how Tania had vanished from the room!

Beatrix and her friends smiled. She said, "This looks like a job for the Cluefinders Club!"

The Cluefinders Club was what the four friends did in their spare time. They loved to play detective. They had all seen Sherlock Holmes on the TV, and thought he was very cool. They had all played computer games with detectives in them, and read plenty of books about children who were also detectives. They wanted to do the same.

So for years they had been meeting after school. They called themselves the Cluefinders Club. There were four members, and it would only ever *have* four members. The best friends would teach themselves how to be detectives, by finding clues and following the trail until the mystery was solved.

All they needed was a real mystery...

...And now they had one!

"The first thing we have to do is establish the facts," said Chris. It was his favourite saying. "Mister Faraday, were you sitting outside the room for the whole time?"

"Yes, that's right," said the teacher, quite amused at the serious children. "I never left that chair."

"And did anyone else enter the room?" asked Ben.

"No, nobody came in or out. I can guarantee it."

"Let's inspect the room," suggested Clara.

Together they checked every inch of the room. There were no hidden doors. There were no squeaky floorboards, hiding a secret tunnel.

"The window is definitely locked," confirmed Clara. "And the store cupboard is definitely empty – except for rulers and pencil sharpeners, of course!"

Chris put his fingers on his chin, thinking. "So, we've confirmed that Tania definitely isn't still in the room, hiding. And there was no way out except for the door. But the door was guarded by Mister Faraday. It really *is* a mystery!"

"Well, I'm stumped," said Mister Faraday, almost ready to give up. "But I hope Tania shows up, otherwise I'm going to have a very awkward conversation with her mother at home time!"

"Don't worry, sir!" said Beatrix confidently. "We'll figure this out before then! We just need some clues..."

"Hang on!" said Ben suddenly. "Are you sure we WANT to find Tania? She's horrible!"

Beatrix laughed. "Yes! Even though she's very mean, we'd better find her and solve this mystery. It's the right thing to do."

Ben went floppy, frowning. "I suppose you're right."

"Look at this!" said Clara. She'd found something.

The store cupboard had a white fingerprint on the door, as if painted there by a tiny brush.

"What's this?"

"Hmm..." said Beatrix, thinking. "What could make a fingerprint like that? It's not food..."

They investigated the cupboard. They found lots of things – empty exercise books for writing in, as well as staplers for stapling, erasers for erasing, and calculators for calculating. They also find some small white bottles marked 'correcting fluid'.

"What's this?" asked Chris, showing the bottle to Mister Faraday.

"Oh, that's just correcting fluid. When you write a mistake, you use it to paint over the incorrect word and write the correct word over the top, once the fluid dries. It's like pressing 'delete' on a computer. We don't use it much nowadays."

Chris opened the bottle. The lid was connected to a tiny brush, that was wet and shiny with white liquid. "Tania must have been messing around in the cupboard, and found a bottle like this! Let's see if we can follow the clues!"

When they examined the room closely, they saw more white fingerprints. Tania had left a trail! They saw white finger prints on the cupboard shelf, the cupboard door, the back of a chair near the window, and then on the wall next to the window itself.

"So Tania played with the correcting fluid and got some on her fingers. Then she went over to the window. Maybe she tried to escape this way?" guessed Clara.

They checked the window. There were two pieces of glass, one at the top and one at the bottom. The bottom part slid up – as long as it was unlocked. There was a little metal lever in the middle that locked and unlocked the window. And there was a white finger print on it!

"Aha!" said Beatrix. "Look – Tania tried to open the window!"

But when they tried to do the same, they found that they couldn't open it. The lock was too stiff.

"I wouldn't bother," Mister Faraday told them, rubbing his moustache with his finger. "That window has been stuck tight for years! Even the teachers can't open it."

"We'd better check, to be sure," said Ben. "I'll look outside!"

So he ran outside and around the building. A minute later, he appeared outside the window. Beatrix waved to him. Smiling, Ben waved back. He looked at the outside of the window. Then he looked at the ground.

When he ran back into the detention room, gasping for breath, he said, "There's no ... footprints outside ... and no ... white fingerprints ... on the window ... Phew!"

"Rest for a while, Ben!" said Beatrix.

Ben had always been the sporty type. He played football and tennis, and was even a member of the local karate team. It didn't take long before he'd gotten his breath back. "No worries! But it looks certain that Tania didn't go out of the window. It was a dead end."

"Then what?" asked Beatrix, looking up at the ceiling. It seemed like they would never solve the mystery. Then she realised: they hadn't checked the ceiling! "Guys, look!"

The ceiling was made up of square white tiles. They were held in place by a metal grid. The children already knew that it was possible to push one of the tiles away so that the empty space in the ceiling was visible. Clara's bedroom, where the Cluefinders Club met most evenings, had the same ones.

"She could have climbed up into the ceiling!" gasped Clara. "Once she was up there, she could have crawled across and dropped down into another room!"

But when Mister Faraday pulled over a chair and climbed up to see, he found that the tiles wouldn't move after all. They were fastened securely in place. He nearly fell off the wobbly chair trying to look!

"It's no good," he told the children after climbing down, wiping sweat off his forehead. "Nobody could get up into the ceiling."

Just then, he gave a long yawn. He covered his mouth with his hand, but it didn't stop his moustache wiggling like a caterpillar. "Yaaa-oooo-oooohm ... Excuse me!"

Beatrix gave him a funny look. "Sorry to ask, sir, but are you tired?"

"Hmm? Oh, a little, I suppose," he replied, adjusting his glasses. "I didn't get much sleep last night. *Somebody* has to mark all that homework, you know!"

"That's it!" said Beatrix, snapping her fingers.

Soon all the other members of the Cluefinders Club got it, too! They had the answer!

Chris said, "Sir, I know you were in the chair the whole lunchtime, reading ... But is it possible that you *fell asleep* for a minute?"

"Fell asleep!" repeated the surprised teacher. "Oh! Ahem. Well, my eyes did get a little heavy there for a while, I suppose ... Yes, it's possible I *might* have nodded off for a moment or two..."

"You fell asleep, and Tania walked right out of the door and sneaked past you!" announced Beatrix. "And I bet I know just where to find her!"

And find her they did: in the classroom, whispering naughtily with Jada and Juliet. She hadn't vanished at all!

"What are *you* idiots looking at?" she snarled, when she saw the Cluefinders Club standing triumphantly in the doorway.

Mister Faraday was very impressed with the four young detectives. "It's no wonder you couldn't figure it out at first – you were making your assumptions on the wrong facts! I'm sorry it never occurred to me before, that I might have fallen asleep in my chair!"

"It's not your fault, sir," laughed Beatrix. "But as punishment for Tania sneaking out of detention, you could always give her more homework!"

Mister Faraday looked shocked. "I suppose you're right! But then I'll *never* get any sleep!"

Beatrix turned to her three best friends: Chris, Ben and Clara. "What do you say, Cluefinders? Mystery solved?"

"Mystery solved!" they all cheered.

And Tania the bully *did* get extra homework that day!

~

**THE END**

~

# ABOUT AUTHOR

# Ken T Seth.

I love to write a customized story or a book for children.

I write inspiration, bed time story for make children smile.

My passion are anything about reading and writing.

Anyone can write but not everyone's word can evoke, depict and change what you want them to.

## Contact

Kindle Page : http://www.amazon.com/Ken-T-Seth/e/B00QSALU46/

Fanpage : https://www.facebook.com/kimaginepub

Website : www.k-imagine-pub.com

# OUR BEST SELLER eBOOKS

Available at :
http://www.amazon.com/Kids-Fantasy-
Books-Unicorn-Bedtime-
ebook/dp/B00WA1MW9Y

THE LITTLE
# MERMAID
Revision Edition

## 2 OPTIONS FOR ENDINGS
### HELP TRAIN CHILDREN'S IMAGINATION
Ken T Seth

## Available at :

http://www.amazon.com/Books-Kids-
Mermaid-Childrens-learning-
ebook/dp/B00R05L0AC

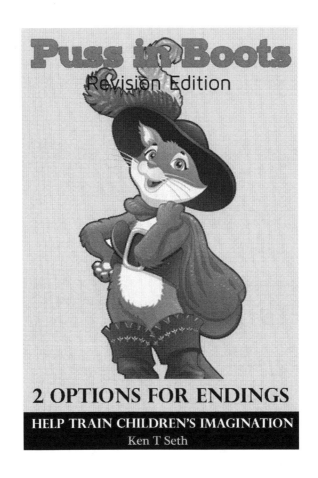

Available at :
http://www.amazon.com/dp/B00R318QO6

# The Wizard of Oz

## Revision Edition

### 2 OPTIONS FOR ENDINGS

HELP TRAIN CHILDREN'S IMAGINATION

Ken T Seth

Available at :

http://www.amazon.com/dp/B00QJGFFAE

# Hansel & Gretel
## Revision Edition

**2 OPTIONS FOR ENDINGS**

**HELP TRAIN CHILDREN'S IMAGINATION**

Ken T Seth

Available at :

www.amazon.com/dp/B00SRU4G9G

## Available at :
www.amazon.com/dp/B00RGYE8NS

Available at :
http://www.amazon.com/dp/B00QJGFFAE

# Peter Pan

## Revision Edition

## 2 OPTIONS FOR ENDINGS

### HELP TRAIN CHILDREN'S IMAGINATION

Ken T Seth

## Available at :
http://www.amazon.com/dp/B00QXFN58A

# THE Frog Prince

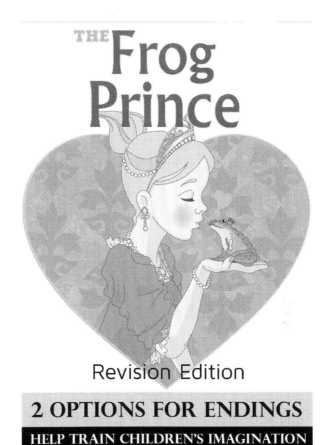

## Revision Edition

## 2 OPTIONS FOR ENDINGS

### HELP TRAIN CHILDREN'S IMAGINATION
Ken T Seth

Available at :
http://www.amazon.com/dp/B00R05UCLA

Made in the USA
San Bernardino, CA
15 September 2017